Aren't You Lucky!

For Tom, Maddy
and Claire

Aren't You Lucky!

❀ Catherine and Laurence Anholt ❀

Red Fox

At first it was me on my own.

Just Mummy and Daddy and me.

I didn't have a little brother then.
I never even thought about it.

Then one day Daddy whispered, "Guess what?
Mummy's going to have another baby. Aren't we lucky!"

"The baby will take a long time to grow inside her," he said. "We'll all have to be very patient."

April

May

June

July

August

September

October

November

December

But I got tired of waiting.

At last the waiting was over. Mummy was going to the hospital.

I didn't want her to go, but I had Granny to look after me.

The next day we all went to visit and . . .

There was
my little brother!

"Aren't you lucky!"
said Granny.

"Do you think he looks like me or like Daddy?" asked Mummy.

"I think he looks like a raspberry," I said.

"Look he's waking up now.

He can't talk yet . . .

but he can cry all right,

especially when he's hungry."

"Can he play with me?"

"No, he's not strong enough
to sit up on his own."

"Hello, little baby," I said.

"Welcome to the world."

After that it was me and my brother.

Mummy and Daddy, my brother and me.

Then lots of people came to see my baby brother,
and they all said, "Aren't you lucky!"

But sometimes
I didn't feel lucky at all.

It took me a long time to get used to that baby.

I always had to wait.

He didn't know how to play.

He cried when
I made music,

but no one got cross
when he made a noise.

Mummy asked me to try to be good, but . . .

I didn't want my tea.

I wanted Mummy to play party with me.

I made myself all spotty.

Sometimes I wanted to be a baby too.

My brother even cried in the bath.

"Thank goodness for a little peace and quiet," said Daddy.

But it didn't
last long!

In the end
Mummy got tired.

"If only I had someone who
could help me," she said.

"I could do that," I said.

As the baby grew bigger,
we found **lots** of ways that I could help.

I make him laugh.

I brush his hair.

I show him my books

and do my jazzy dance.

There were all kinds of things
we could do **together** . . .

Going for a walk.

Watching TV.

Having a bath

and a bedtime cuddle.

Now he likes me
best of all.

And whenever people see me with my little brother, they say,

"Isn't he lucky!"

AREN'T YOU LUCKY!
A RED FOX BOOK 978 1 782 95230 5
First published in Great Britain by The Bodley Head, an imprint of Random House Children's Publishers UK
A Penguin Random House Company

Penguin
Random House
UK

The Bodley Head edition published 1990
Red Fox edition published 1992
This Red Fox edition with new illustrations published 2015.

1 3 5 7 9 10 8 6 4 2

Copyright © Catherine and Laurence Anholt, 1990, 2015

The right of Laurence and Catherine Anholt to be identified as author and illustrator of this work has been asserted in accordance
with the Copyright, Designs and Patents Act 1988.

All rights reserved. Set in ChimpAndZee

Red Fox Books are published by Random House Children's Publishers UK,
61-63 Uxbridge Road, London W5 5SA

www.randomhousechildrens.co.uk   www.randomhouse.co.uk

Addresses for companies within The Random House Group Limited can be found at:
www.randomhouse.co.uk/offices.htm

THE RANDOM HOUSE GROUP Limited Reg. No. 954009

A CIP catalogue record for this book is available from the British Library.

Printed in China

The Random House Group Limited supports the Forest Stewardship Council® (FSC®), the leading international
forest-certification organisation. Our books carrying the FSC label are printed on FSC®-certified paper.
FSC is the only forest-certification scheme endorsed by the leading environmental organizations, including Greenpeace.
Our paper procurement policy can be found at www.randomhouse.co.uk/environment.

MIX
Paper from
responsible sources
FSC® C104723